THE
THANKSGIVING DAY
FROM THE
BLACK LAGOON

HA, HA, HA. HA. HA.

Get more monster-sized laughs from

The Black Lagoon

THE
THANKSGIVING DAY
FROM THE
BLACK LAGOON

DO YOU HAVE PLANS FOR THE HOLIDAY?

by Mike Thaler
Illustrated by Jared Lee

SCHOLASTIC INC.

New York Toronto London Auckland
Sydney Mexico City New Delhi Hong Kong

MINI
PIGEON →
(EXACT SIZE)

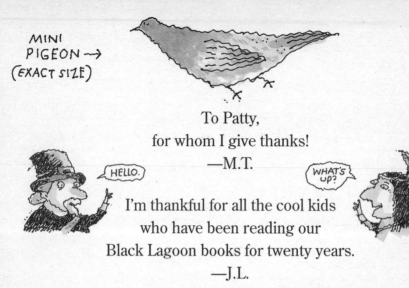

To Patty,
for whom I give thanks!
—M.T.

HELLO.

WHAT'S UP?

I'm thankful for all the cool kids
who have been reading our
Black Lagoon books for twenty years.
—J.L.

ISBN-13: 978-0-545-16812-0
ISBN-10: 0-545-16812-0

Text copyright © 2009 by Mike Thaler
Illustrations copyright © 2009 by Jared D. Lee Studio, Inc.

All rights reserved. Published by Scholastic Inc.

SCHOLASTIC, LITTLE APPLE, and associated logos are trademarks and/or
registered trademarks of Scholastic Inc. BLACK LAGOON is a registered
trademark of Mike Thaler and Jared D. Lee Studio, Inc. All rights reserved.
Lexile is a registered trademark of MetaMetrics, Inc.

12 11 10 9 8 7 6   11 12 13 14/0

Printed in the U.S.A.
First printing, October 2009

CONTENTS

CHAPTER 1
FOR THE BIRDS

It's November. There's a chill in the air. The frost is on the pumpkin and the pumpkin is in the pie. Our class is excited about vacation, but our teacher is excited about learning.

"Who knows what holiday is coming up?" asks Mrs. Green.

Derek's hand shoots up. "Fall!" he shouts.

"Fall is a season, not a holiday." Mrs. Green smiles.

FOOT → BALL →

Eric's hand shoots up.

"Football!" he shouts.

"Football is a sport, not a holiday."

Penny raises her hand and waits to be called on.

"Yes, Penny?" says Mrs. Green.

"The holiday that is rapidly approaching is Thanksgiving." She smiles and puts her hand down.

SIGN OF CONFIDENCE →

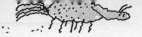

"That's right, Penny, and where was the first Thanksgiving?" asks Mrs. Green.

Derek's hand shoots up. "In Turkey," he shouts out.

"*You're* a turkey," snickers Eric. "It started in Greece."

"It was a greasy turkey," retorts Derek.

"Now, boys, you're both wrong—who knows the correct answer?"

Penny waves her hand in the air.

"Yes, Penny," says Mrs. Green. "Thanksgiving is a uniquely American holiday that was first celebrated in New England in 1621."

"I knew that," says Derek.

"What are some things you enjoy about Thanksgiving?" asks Mrs. Green.

"We don't have to come to school," shouts out Eric without raising his hand.

CHAPTER 2
THANKS A LOT

Mrs. Green smiles. "There are a lot of good things about Thanksgiving. We enjoy good food. The Thanksgiving Day parade is fun to watch. But most of all, it's a chance for us to give thanks for all the good things we have."

← ERIC

"Like football," says Eric.
"Well, football is certainly one of them." Mrs. Green laughs.

← FOOTBALL

17

Penny raises her hand.
"Yes, Penny?"
"Could we have a Thanksgiving Day parade of our own?" she asks.
"Good idea!" says Mrs. Green.
"With floats and costumes?" asks Penny.

"That's a great idea!" says Mrs. Green. "Who knows how to make a float?"

Derek's hand shoots up.

"It's easy," says Derek. "You need two scoops of vanilla ice cream and one can of root beer."

STRAW

ROOT BEER

COLD MUG

ICE CREAM

VANILLA PREFERRED

HOW TO MAKE A FLOAT

DEMONSTRATION

CHAPTER 3
FLOATING ALONE

When everybody stops laughing and Derek has left for the principal's office, we choose teams to make our floats.

"I choose Doris," says Penny.

"Of chorus," says Eric. "And I choose Derek."

COME IN, DEREK, I'VE BEEN EXPECTING YOU.

OH, GREAT.

PRINCIPAL

21

Well, that hurt. Randy chooses Freddy, and no one chooses me.

"Hubie, whose team would you like to be on?" asks Mrs. Green.

"I don't want to be on anybody's team," I answer. "I'm a team of one."

NO TEAM? NO PROBLEM.

23

CHAPTER 4
TEAMING UP

On the school bus home, each float team is busy making their float plans.

BIG MOUTH DOG ↙

25

"We'll have a ballet dancer," says Doris, who loves to show off her tutu.

"We'll make a giant football," say Eric and Derek.

"We'll make a big turkey," say Freddy and Randy.

"And what will you make?" everyone asks, looking at me.

"I'll make up my mind about what to make when I am good and ready," I say, looking out the window.

BLAH, BLAH. BLAH.

WHAT AM I GOING TO DO?

BLAH, BLAH. BLAH.

26

OTHER FLOAT IDEAS

LEFTOVERS

27

CHAPTER 5
A GUY'S BEST FRIEND

When I get home, I tell Mom the whole story.

"What do you want your float to
be?" she asks.

"Easy," I answer.

"The easy way is not always the best way," she says. "I'll be on your team, Hubie, and our float will win first prize."

Oh, great. Now I have a team that wants to overachieve.

OTHER BIRD OPTIONS FOR THE THANKSGIVING DINNER

OWL

SWAN

EAGLE

OSTRICH

FLAMINGO

PENGUIN

VULTURE

PARROT

31

CHAPTER 6

DOING THE CAN-CAN

"We could make a float about saving the environment," says Mom. "It can show the things we should recycle, like bottles, paper, and cans."

"It sounds like a garbage truck to me," I say.

"There's an idea!" says Mom. "We could make a big trash can."

"That's too messy. Let's just make a big soup can instead."

"We could," says Mom.

"We can!" I say.

NOODLE ⟶

And so we start on our float. We take two hula hoops and connect them with sticks. Then we wrap the sticks with butcher paper. It looks like a giant can. Now we need to paint it.

"Let's make it chicken soup," says Mom.

"Let's make it turkey noodle," I say, "since it's a Thanksgiving Day parade."

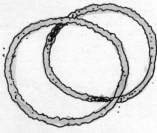

HULA HOOPS

STICKS

GLUE

BUTCHER PAPER

TAPE

CHAPTER 7
THE PARADERS OF THE LOST PARK

So that's what we do. We get paint and brushes. I paint one side of the can while Mom paints the other.

MOM, I HAVE THE PAINT. CAN YOU GRAB THE BRUSHES?

37

ANSWER: SHIP

On Wednesday morning we put the can on my wagon and I pull it to school.

DON'T DROP IT, MOM.

All the other teams are there with their floats. Doris stands in a wagon wearing her tutu while Penny pulls her around the playground. Freddy and Randy made a big turkey out of papier-mâché, but it looks more like the Loch Ness monster with feathers. Eric and Derek stand together in a giant Giants' football jersey and hold a football.

LOCH NESS
MONSTER ⟶

SCOTLAND
↓

39

My can wins hands down—or really, hands up. Everyone votes for me except Eric and Derek. Eric and Derek only have one vote, anyway, since they are standing in the same shirt.

Mrs. Green pins a big blue ribbon on my can and the parade goes on.

40

41

CHAPTER 8
PLYMOUTH ROCKS

After the parade, Mrs. Beamster reads us a book about the first Thanksgiving. We learn how the Native Americans helped the new settlers to survive. The Native Americans taught the settlers how to plant corn and to hunt for wild turkeys so that they would have enough food for the winter.

There were no supermarkets then—no markets at all. We really do have a lot to be thankful for.

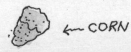

That afternoon when Mom and I go shopping for a turkey, sweet potatoes, fresh cranberries, and apple cider, I give thanks in every aisle.

NO, HUBIE, THE TURKEY WASN'T WILD. IT WAS RAISED ON A TURKEY RANCH.

WITH COWBOYS ON HORSES?

THE HISTORY OF THANKSGIVING

THE PILGRIMS CROSSED THE OCEAN ON THE __MAYFLOWER__.

THEY LANDED AT PLYMOUTH ROCK AND BUILT SMALL CABINS WITHIN A FORT.

ONE DAY THE NATIVE AMERICANS STOPPED BY TO INTRODUCE THEMSELVES. THEY THOUGHT THE PILGRIMS WERE FROM MARS.

THE PILGRIMS WERE NOT GOOD HUNTERS...

...OR FARMERS.

THE NATIVE AMERICANS SAW THIS AND DECIDED TO HELP. THEY TOLD THEM ABOUT WILD TURKEYS AND HOW TO GROW CORN.

IN THE FALL THE PILGRIMS, THANKFUL FOR THEIR BOUNTIFUL HARVEST, INVITED THEIR NEW FRIENDS TO A DAY OF FEAST AND FELLOWSHIP. THEY CALLED THE CELEBRATION THANKSGIVING.

CHAPTER 9

LET'S TALK TURKEY

I begin to feel sorry for the turkeys. They don't look forward to Thanksgiving the way we do. I wonder if they have calendars and cross off the days.

That night I have a nightmare. I dream that I am a turkey and as the days grow shorter, so does my life. I hope everyone will become a vegetarian.

47

Then all we turkeys are playing football. It is the Turkey Bowl. They throw me the ball and I'm being chased by a giant can of turkey noodle soup. Luckily, I wake up before it tackles me.

Boy, I think, *we* do *have a lot to be thankful for.*

49

CHAPTER 10
THE RIGHT STUFF

On Thanksgiving Day I eat a lot. In fact, I eat too much. I have too much turkey, too much stuffing, too many mashed potatoes, too many sweet potatoes, too many string beans, too many peas, and too many carrots. Then when I can hardly move, I have dessert—pumpkin pie with peppermint ice cream.

THANKSGIVING DINNER
PLUS DESSERT

51

After dinner I am really thankful for Pepto-Bismol and the fact that Thanksgiving only comes once a year.

53

CHAPTER 11

COME RIGHT OVER FOR LEFTOVERS

Which brings us to leftovers. We have turkey sandwiches, turkey casserole, turkey soup, turkey burgers, turkey tacos, and turkey pizza.

HONEY, I'M WORKING LATE TONIGHT, SO FIX YOURSELF A TURKEY SANDWICH. THERE'S ALSO A LOT OF TURKEY SALAD AND TURKEY PIE, SO MAKE SURE YOU EAT THAT, TOO.

NOT AGAIN.

SIGNED BASEBALL ←

55

We eat turkey something almost every day into the new year. I don't want to look another turkey in the eye till next Thanksgiving rolls around. By then, almost everyone in America will be getting stuffed again, along with their turkeys.

WHAT HOLIDAY DO WE CELEBRATE IN NOVEMBER?

CHRISTMAS

FOURTH OF JULY

EASTER

HALLOWEEN

THANKSGIVING

MIKE THALER'S BIRTHDAY

57

ANSWER ON PAGE 60

61

ANSWER ON PAGE 63

WHAT ARE YOU THANKFUL FOR?

1. _____
2. _____
3. _____
4. _____
5. _____
6. _____
7. _____
8. _____
9. _____
10. _____
11. _____
12. _____